富士山

MT. FUJI

大山行男

MT. FUJI

photographs by

Yukio Ohyama

with essays by

Makoto Ōoka

C. W. Nicol

Hitoshi Takeuchi

E. P. DUTTON   NEW YORK

First published, 1987, in the United States by E. P. Dutton, New York. / Copyright © 1984 by Yukio Ohyama / Q Photo International. / All rights reserved. / No part of this publication may be reproduced or transmitted in any form or by any means, electronic or mechanical, including photocopy, recording or any information storage and retrieval system now known or to be invented, without permission in writing from the publisher, except by a reviewer who wishes to quote brief passages in connection with a review written for inclusion in a magazine, newspaper or broadcast. / Published in Japan by Graphic-sha Publishing Co., Ltd., Tokyo. / Published in the United States by E. P. Dutton, a division of New American Library, 2 Park Avenue, New York, N.Y. 10016. / Published simultaneously in Canada by Fitzhenry & Whiteside Limited, Toronto. / Library of Congress Catalog Card Number: 86-72462. / ISBN: 0-525-24517-0 / CUSA / Printed and bound in Japan. / 10 9 8 7 6 5 4 3 2 1 / First Edition

CONTENTS

THE JAPANESE AND MT. FUJI

Makoto Ōoka

(Poet)

Because I was born in Mishima in Izu, which is connected to the southern base of Mt. Fuji, Fuji was for me part of the home that I was used to seeing every day. The image of Fuji early in the morning on a fine day, when the silhouette of Mt. Hōei floats especially clearly, is distinctly etched in my mind even now, when I have been living in Tokyo for a long time. Mt. Hōei is Fuji's parasite volcano formed during the 1704 eruption. The top has a gigantic cavity. As a child, it was amusing to gaze at it and think that the deformity accented Fuji like a navel.

Mt. Fuji has been extolled in poetry dating back to the *Manyoshu*. Generations of Japanese have paid it reverence beyond that given to an ordinary volcano. In the third book of the *Manyoshu*, the two *choka* (long poems) and three *hanka* (short ancillary poems), grouped together praising Mt. Fuji, stand out. One is that famous poem by Yamabe no Akahito that reads:

> The Tago coast
> Going forth, I gaze
> Such pure whiteness
> The snow on Fuji's towering peak

However, as a poem extolling the incomparable majesty of Mt. Fuji, the anonymous *choka* that follows this one is far more impressive. The imposing appearance of Fuji rising between Kai and Suruga provinces is introduced at the beginning. It then continues:

> Clouds in the sky
> Are kept from going forth
> Birds that fly
> Fly but cannot fly so high
> Burning fires
> Are quenched by snow
> Falling snow
> Melts in the fire
> It cannot be expressed
> It cannot be named
> How divine
> This god
>
> The god protects
> The land of Yamato
> The source of the sun
> A treasure
> This god
> In Suruga
> One never tires of gazing
> At the towering peak of Fuji
> (Book Three, 319)

This is impressive as a succinct description of Mt. Fuji during the eighth and ninth centuries, when the volcano was active and erupted frequently at twenty- to thirty-year intervals. The people of the *Manyōshu* period thought of Fuji, the mountain spouting fire, as an inexplicable god, "How divine/This god." Their feelings of praise, "protects/ The land of Yamato/The source of the sun" can easily be understood. They must have been filled with awe for the most beautiful mountain in Japan that erupted repeatedly, as well as uneasiness and fear of the mountain that could cause a major disaster.

This *choka* must have been written around the beginning of the eighth century. About 150 years later, however, during the early part of the Heian Period, the attitude toward Fuji became very detailed. Descriptions appeared that make one wonder how something so detailed could have been written. Representative of this is the *Account of Fuji* (*Honchō Monzui*) in *kanbun* (Chinese read in a Japanese way) written by Miyako no Yoshika, a scholarly man of letters. "Mt. Fuji is in the province of Suruga. The peak looks as if it has been shaved. Towering in simple solitude, it reaches for the heavens. Its height is beyond measure. Looking over all the historical places recorded, there has never been a mountain to this day higher than this one," he begins. He then continues, "At the summit is some level ground about 2.44 miles wide. In the center of the peak is a cavity shaped like a cooking pot (a pot for steaming). At the bottom of the pot is a divine pond. In the middle of the pond is a large rock. The shape of the rock is amazing. It is just like a crouching tiger. Also in the pot there is always a mist steaming forth. The color is pure blue." And so forth.

Writing as if he had actually seen the event, Yoshika tells us that long ago someone called En no Gyōja managed to climb to the summit of Fuji. It is amusing that En no Gyōja's name is always referred to at such times, but it is interesting to learn that a description of looking into the crater of Mt. Fuji already existed in ninth-century writings.

Since then, Fuji has been celebrated not only in poetry and prose. By how many brushes has Mt. Fuji been painted by artists ranging from Hokusai and Hiroshige to Yokoyama Taikan and Umehara Ryūzaburo down through the modern painters. I, myself, have not yet written a poem about Mt. Fuji. Perhaps this is because it was too close to me during my youth. However, it is probably because Mt. Fuji is closer to me in a form quite different from the shape of the mountain. For me Mt. Fuji was first "water" rather than anything else.

Thus the Fuji that is the most familiar and nostalgic to me is the water from the melted snow on the mountain that passes through the rock beds deep in the earth and gushes forth in the western and northern parts of the town of Mishima. The water is plentiful, and it is in this clear river water that I have my Fuji. Once when asked, "What does Mt. Fuji mean to you?" I answered, "Mt. Fuji is water." My questioner was momentarily taken aback but then understood as soon as I explained.

One's home lives within one in a form inconceivable to someone born in another place. I feel certain that Mt. Fuji exists in a variety of forms in each Japanese. That surely is the real meaning behind the frequent use of Mt. Fuji as a symbol of Japan.

From Misaka Pass AM7:20

▶ From Asagiri Heights AM7:40

◂From Mt. Tou in Tanzawa AM6:30

From Jūrigi AM6:10

9

◂ From Jūrigi AM9:30

From Nagao Pass in Hakone PM10:00

From Ashigara Pass in Hakone PM5:30

▶ At the First Station of Fuji Forest Road   AM10:30

◢ From the sky above the Fifth Station, Fujinomiya Side   AM8:20

From the sky above Lake Yamanaka   AM10:50

◀From the sky above Gotemba Entrance AM10:00

From Mt. Mitsutōge AM7:30

20

From Mt. Ishiwari   AM5:10

▶From Mt. Mitsutōge   AM4:00

From Asagiri Heights   AM7:40

From Lake Motosu AM6:35

▶ From Mt. Takazasu AM7:30

25

◀ From Mt. Amari AM6:20

From Mt. Kushigata AM7:55

◁ From Mt. Ogōchi of the Japan Alps PM8:45

From Mt. Warusawa of the Japan Alps AM6:40

From the sky above Lake Sagami   AM10:15

A Cherry Tree in Ōasumi AM10:00

From Heta in Izu Peninsula   AM9:00

35

From Mitsu Pass   AM8:00

From Lake Ashinoko   AM8:00

◀ From Mt. Kōmori of the Japan Alps AM5:30

From Inogashira Forest Road AM6:00

From Mt. Hōō of the Japan Alps   PM7:00

A GIFT FROM THE MOUNTAIN

C. W. Nicol

(Novelist)

As a boy, fond of books, I had read of a high volcano called "Fujiyama." Just before coming to Japan I read a book by "a famous world traveler" in which the famous man explained that the Japanese so respected Mt. Fuji that they used the honorific for humans, calling the mountain "Fuji-san" (Mr. Fuji).

That's a simple mistake if you don't read *kanji*, for the Japanese do have a special respect for their highest and most perfect mountain, and this has been noticed by the rest of the world.

As the end of my third Arctic expedition drew to a close, and I talked of plans to visit Japan, a comrade said that he had an ambition to climb Mt. Fuji and gaze into the crater, as he had never seen a photograph of the inside.

"I'll get there first," I boasted with a laugh.

I came to Japan in October 1962. That December news came that my friend had fallen into a crevasse in Antarctica and that his body could not be found. My New Year's resolution then was to climb up Mt. Fuji and gaze into the crevasse—for him.

I left on January 3, 1963. Coming from the Arctic I had excellent cold-weather gear. From Fujiyoshida I walked alone up to Station Five and there stayed the night with the lovely old man and his wife, who ran the station, and several young climbers. I spoke perhaps a hundred words of Japanese.

Vivid memories were imprinted on my mind of sitting around the *kotatsu* while the wind howled outside and cold bit at the walls. I was savoring mountain friendship, new-tasting tidbits, and warmed sake.

An awful stink came up from under the kotatsu quilts. Suddenly, my foot hurt and I jerked it out, smoldering. I'd been digging my thickly socked toes into the brazier of charcoal. How everybody laughed!

That morning the weather was fine, but as I got ready to leave the old man seized my arm, pointing to my boots and shaking his head. Other climbers made me understand. I had no climbing spikes, and it was too dangerous.

Dejected but not defeated, I returned that day to Tokyo and went shopping for climbing spikes, or crampons. Two days later I was back at Station Five.

The weather had worsened but I tried, alone again. High winds almost blew me off the steep slopes, and clouds and drifting snow obscured vision and stung my face. Arctic veteran though I was, the mountain scorned me.

I trudged back to Fujiyoshida, miserable. I had only enough money left to get back on the train. As I got to the edge of the town I stopped to unlash the crampons—there, stuck to them, was a folded one-thousand-yen note! A gift from the mountain—for there was no way I could find the owner.

Luck led me to a small *minshuku* where I showed the note and explained in jerky Japanese that it was all I had. They made me welcome, fed me like a prince, and I drank sake all evening with the owner and his wife. My depression at failure lifted a little. I would come back!

When I drew back the wooden *amado* in the morning I gasped. Mt. Fuji was framed in glistening perfection in the window, smiling at me from a blue, blue sky.

I had to go back to Tokyo, but I did return, and got to the summit on January 15, 1963. I looked down into the crater and over the vista—the panorama of Japan—and said a little prayer for my expedition comrade.

Now, every time I return to Japan, my home now, I peer eagerly out of the plane window, trying to get a glimpse of that dangerous, generous, lovely mountain that beckons to all who love Japan.

Torii(a Shrine gate)at the top of Mt. Fuji AM7:00

From the sky above Fujinomiya　AM11:20

▶ From Kengamine　AM4:00

The Crater of Mt. Fuji from Mt. Mishima PM0:30

▶ From Kengamine AM3:50

At the top of Mt. Fuji PM2:00

▶ At the top of Mt. Fuji PM2:30

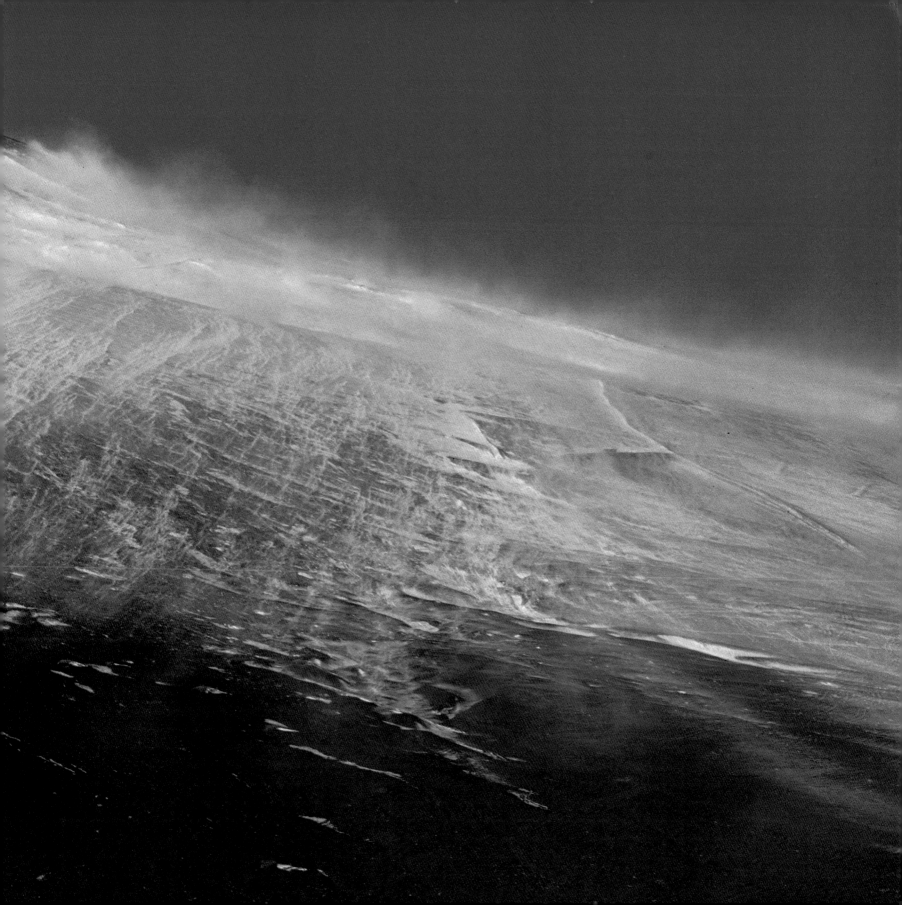

◀ From Futatsuzuka of Gotemba Entrance AM11:00

From Kagosaka Pass PM11:00

From Narusawa Village　AM9:10

55

From Futatsuzuka of Gotemba Entrance   AM11:30

From Mt. Hōei AM9:00

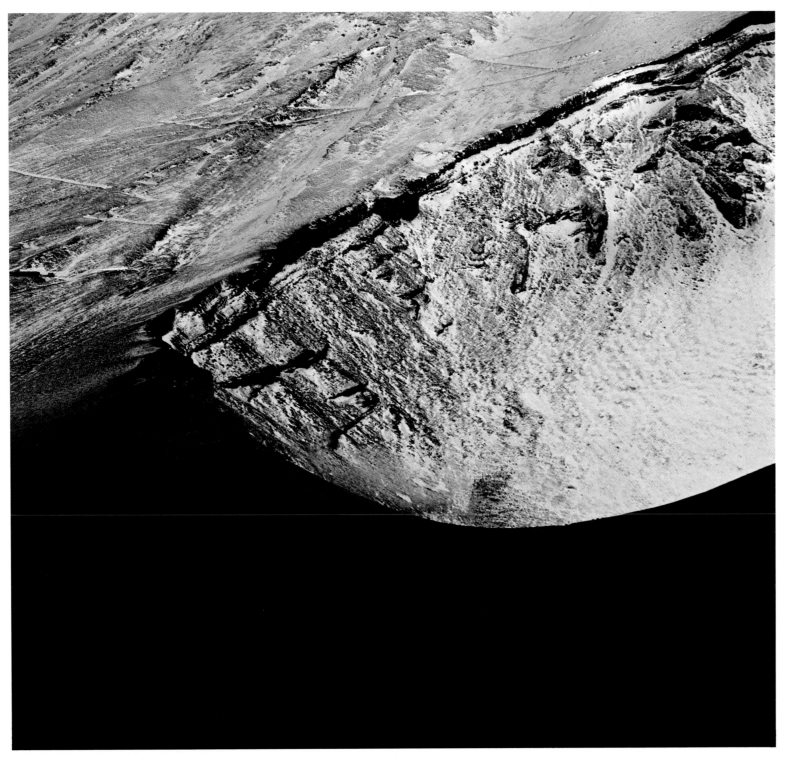

◀ The Crater of Mt. Hōei from Sekotsuji PM5:20

The Crater of Mt. Hōei from Mizugatsuka AM6:50

Gotemba Climbing Road and the Crater of Mt. Hoei   AM11:00

The Crater of Mt. Hoei　AM8:00

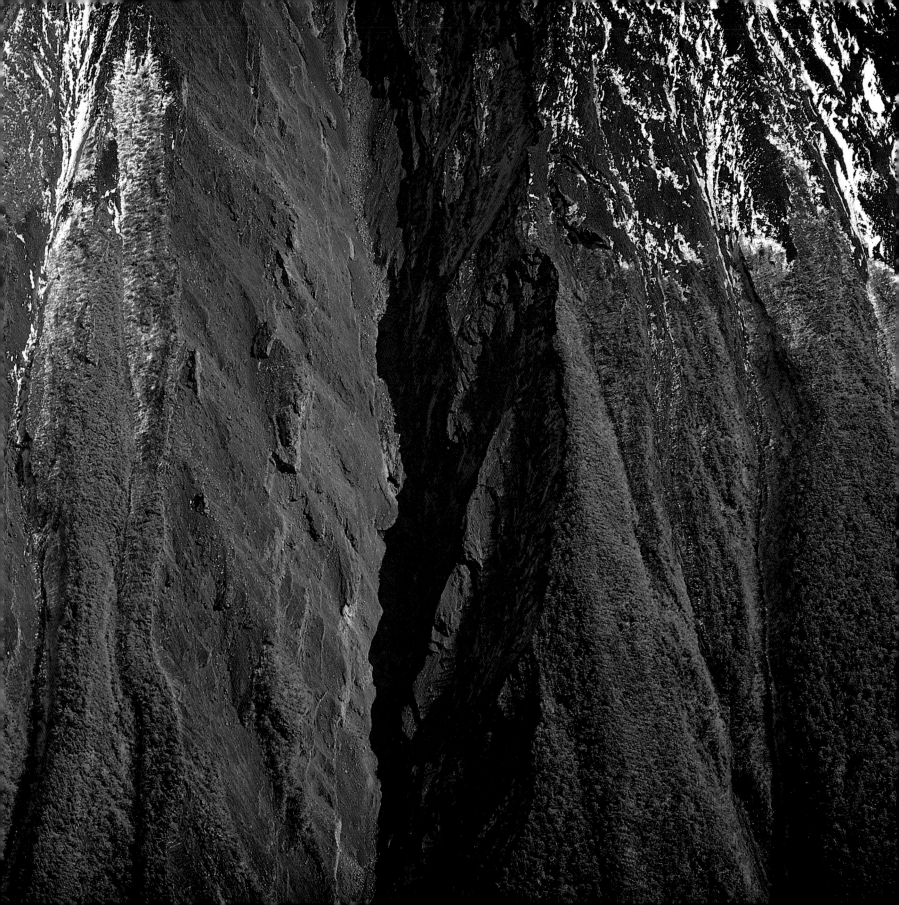

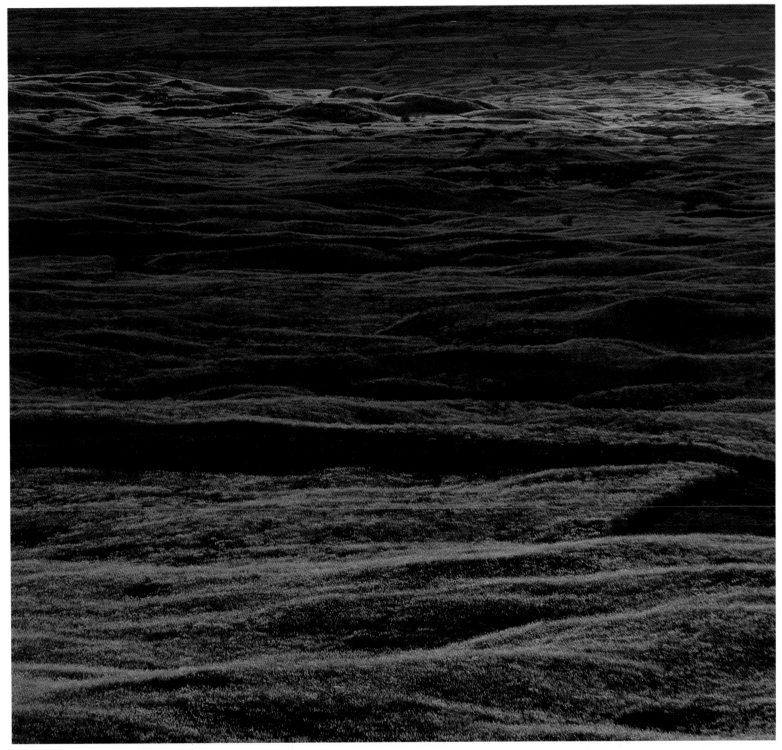

◄ Mountatin Stream of the West Side AM9:00

At Hiratsuka, the east foot of Mt. Fuji AM6:40

At Gotemba Entrance AM8:00

At Kagosaka Pass   PM4:00

65

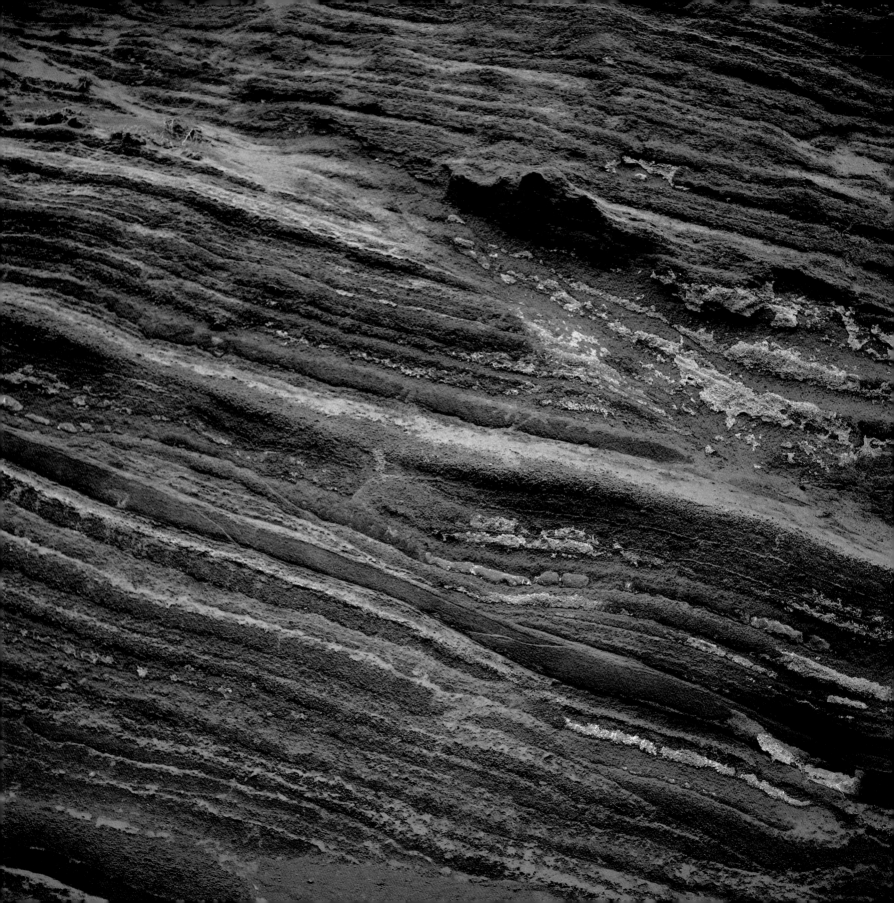

Fault　AM10:00

Lava　PM5:00

At Subashiri Fifth Station, after rain AM11:00

MT. FUJI

Hitoshi Takeuchi
(Professor Emeritus, Tokyo University)

The present Mt. Fuji, which was formed as a result of a third volcanic eruption, is approximately 10,000 years old. It covers an older Mt. Fuji called Ko-fuji in Japanese. This second Mt. Fuji was active about 50,000 to 60,000 years ago. Under this second Mt. Fuji we have the original mountain, which was known as Mt. Komitake. This first volcanic mountain was active 500,000 to 600,000 years ago.

When we look up Mt. Fuji from the Lake Kawaguchi side (north side of the mountain) we can see a mountain shape, the top of which is the end of the Subaru Line. It extends to 5-*gōme* (five tenths the height of Mt. Fuji). The western part of this mountain shape appears different from other portions. The reason is that it is part of the first active volcano, Mt. Komitake. At the crater of Mt. Hōei there are red rocks called Aka-iwa. These are part of the older Mt. Fuji, the second volcano, which resulted after the Hōei eruption.

The present Mt. Fuji is only 10,000 years old and it is still alive. Since A.D. 800, the beginning of the Heian Era in Japanese history, it has been recorded in history books that Mt. Fuji has erupted as many as fourteen times—in A.D. 781, 800, 826, 864, (the fourth year of Jōgan according to the Japanese calendar), 870, 932, 937, 999, 1033, 1083, 1511, 1560, 1700, and again in 1707 (the sixth year of Hōei). From the Shizuoka Prefecture side, which is the south side, we can see a hump on the right side. This hump gives the mountain a somewhat unbalanced appearance. Actually, this "hump" is Mt. Hōei, which is a parasitic volcano formed during the Hōei eruption. This eruption is described in detail in Hakuseki Arai's autobiography, *Oritaku Shiba No Ki*.

During the eruption in Jōgan 6 (A.D. 864), Aokigahara lava extruding from Mt. Nagao, a parasitic volcano on Mt. Fuji, flew into the lake called Woman's Sea. This caused the lake to be divided into three parts. These three parts are now known as Lake Motosu, Lake Shoji, and Lake Sai. The lava flowing out of Mt. Nagao created a broad land of lava. Because the lava-made soil was moist, the land turned into a huge jungle. This jungle is now known as Aokigahara Jukai (sea of leafage). It is said that once people enter this jungle, they will never return. The jungle is only 1,000 years old. In addition to the three previously mentioned lakes, there are two more—Lake Kawaguchi and Lake Yamanaka. Together we call these Fuji-go-ko, which means "five lakes." These lakes all lie at the northern foot of Mt. Fuji. Each lake is a so-called dam lake. This is because they were dammed by the lava during the eruption of the present Mr. Fuji. As for the age of these lakes, Lake Kawaguchi is the oldest, 5,000 to 7,000 years old. All the others are less than 2,000 years old. Oshino Village, located on the northwest side of Lake Yamanaka, is three square kilometers of flat land. Several thousand years ago, this flat land was the bottom of Lake Oshino, which had been formed by the lava dam. Lake Oshino later dried up and became the present flat village.

For example, Aokigahara-Maruo was formed by the hardened lava from the Jōgan eruption. Steam extruding from the inside of the earth smashed lava blocking the crater or part of the mountain and scattered the pieces about.

These pieces became known as "ejecta." Subashiri is where these ejecta were piled the deepest. During an earthquake, a thaw, a heavy rain, and so forth, these ejecta sometimes slide down the side of the mountain. This is known as a "volcanic muddy stream."

At Taishaku-ji or other places at the southwest foot of Mt. Fuji, this volcanic-mud stream bed is broadly spread. On the surface of Mt. Fuji, there are many tunnels called "ice holes" or "wind holes." These holes were made because the outer layer of the flowing lava hardened faster than the inner layer. A lava leafage, which we can often see in the Aokigahara leafage sea, is a hole that was formed after a tree was surrounded by a lava stream causing the inside to evaporate. In the southern part of the Kantō Plain, thick volcanic ash has accumulated forming the so-called Kantō Loam Stratum. This stratum has been formed from the ejecta that had drifted with the west wind from the older Mt. Fuji volcano to the Kantō Plain and had been piling up there until now.

Lava stream or ejecta from Mt. Fuji have a lot of cracks or holes. As a result, water penetrates them easily. Therefore, most of the rain on Mt. Fuji is absorbed into the mountain's body, flows down the volcanic-mud stream bed on the older Mt. Fuji, then moves along the bed surface and then finally wells out at the foot of Mt. Fuji. The water in the Mt. Fuji lakes and Shraito Falls and the industrial water used by factories in the surrounding area is welled out this same way.

At the top of Mt. Fuji, a weather station has been operating since 1936. The annual average temperature at the top is 6.6 degrees below zero centigrade. Air pressure is two-thirds that of the plain. When air rises along the slope of Mt. Fuji, a *kasagumo* (hat-shaped cloud) is formed when the air expands and cools. People living around Mt. Fuji believe that if a kasagumo appears on Mt. Fuji, there will be rain.

The highest part of Mt. Fuji is 12,388 feet above sea level. Botanically, it is called "high mountain zone." Unlike the high zones of many other mountains, Mt. Fuji has no creeping pine, no alpine plants, no alpine animal-like starmigans, Yachi-nezumi (a kind of wild mouse), Azumitogari-nezumi (another kind of wild mouse), or Kōzan-chō (alpine butterfly). This means that Mt. Fuji is a new volcano.

At the top of Mt. Fuji there is a Sengen-jinja (shrine) where the spirits of medieval samurais are gathered. Many beautiful Mt. Fujis can be seen in *Taketori Tale* or *Manyōshū* (poetry) written in the ninth century, and in the great series of landscape prints created in the nineteenth century by Hokusai Katsushika (*Thirty-six Views of Mt. Fuji*) and by Hiroshige Andō (*The Fifty-three Stations of the Tokaido*).

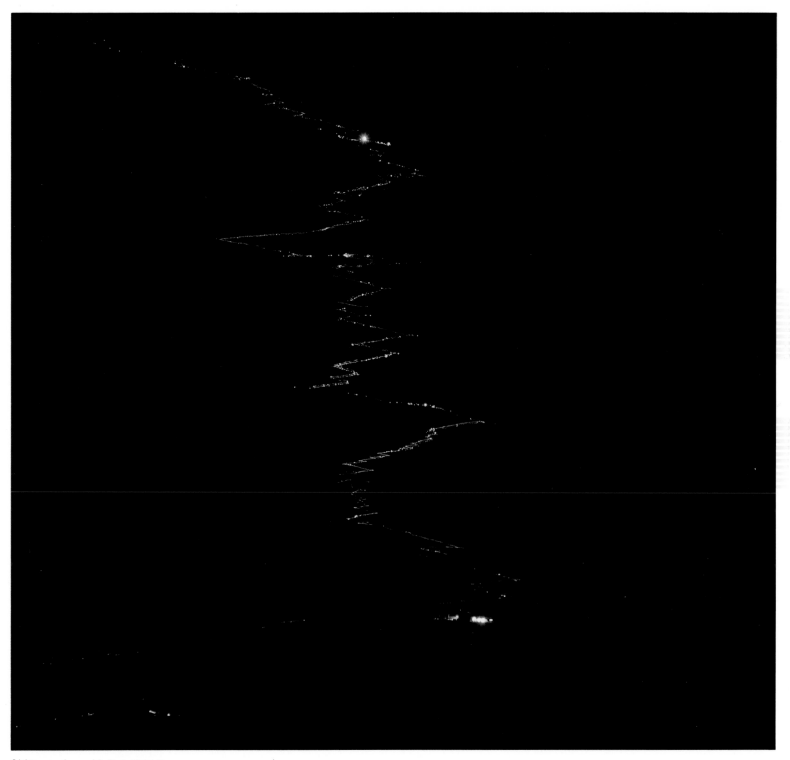

Lights are going up Mt. Fuji   PM11:00

◀At Osawa Fifth Station AM9:00

At Motomurayama AM11:00

At Sengen Shrine in Fujiyoshida AM10:30

▶ In Mt. Ōmuro AM11:00

76

At the Second Station of Fuji Forest Road   AM9:00

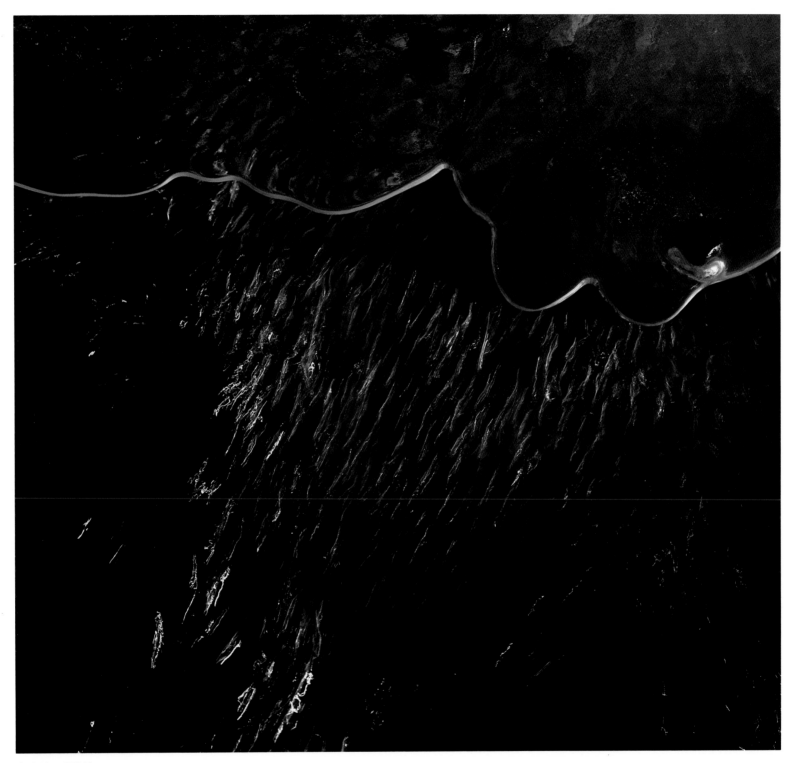

At Oshino AM9:00

At the Third Station of Fuji Forest Road   AM8:00

At the Third Station of Fuji Forest Road AM8:30

A mountain hut at Subashiri Seventh Station   AM8:00

Lake Yamanaka from a hut at Subashiri Seventh Station   AM4:30

Fujiyoshida in lightning   PM9:00

Shōnan seashore from Hiratsuka   AM5:00

From Mt. Kushigata   AM6:30

From Mt. Mitsutōge   AM6:20

From Mt. Hirogōchi of the Japan Alps AM8:00

From Mt. Ogōchi of the Japan Alps   AM5:20

From Mt. Ogōchi of the Japan Alps   AM4:40

From Lake Motosu   AM6:20

From Asagiri Heights   PM5:35

From outskirts of Fujinomiya   PM10:00

From Mt. Mitsutōge   AM4:00

From Mt. Mitsutōge   PM8:00

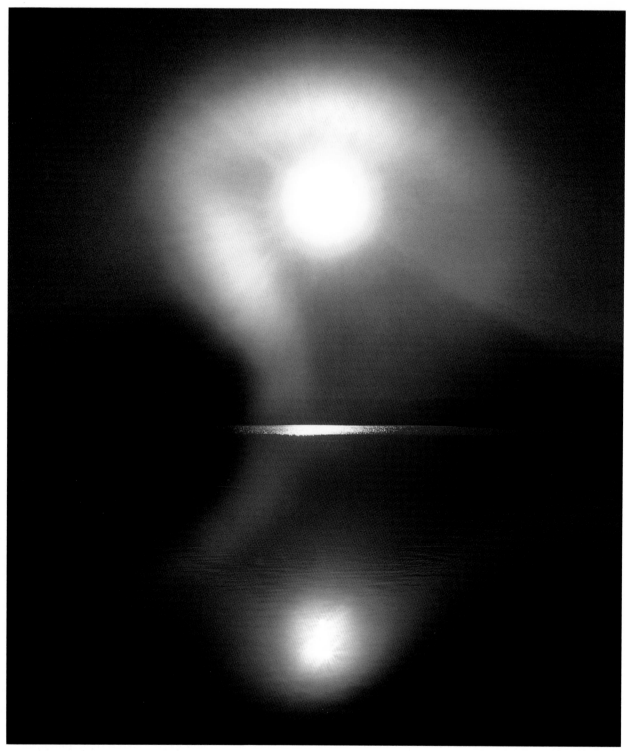

From Lake Tanuki AM6:00

AFTERWORD

Yukio Ohyama
(Photographer)

I was born in Odawara, but at the beginning of my elementary schooling my family moved to a hill in Yokohama. From this eminence I have been viewing Mt. Fuji both mornings and evenings ever since. The peak, standing clearly and serenely above the furrowed ridges of Tanzawa Mountain on a bright winter day, has never failed to be an inspiring sight to me.

A feeling of special attachment to Mt. Fuji came over me one late December day eight years ago while leafing through an album of photographs. The pictures were all of Mt. Fuji taken from a variety of angles, heights, and hours. Opened up for me were exciting new vistas of the mountain, entirely different from the silhouette with which I was so familiar.

Since that day I have been obsessed with the feeling that one of the assignments of my life is to find the best way to grasp and understand this mountain.

Consequently, at the beginning of the new year I climbed Mt. Mitsutōge to take my first pictures of Mt. Fuji. To my delight, hoarfrost clothed Mt. Fuji's slopes. The pure white crystals reflected, glittered, and scattered in the morning sunlight. How lucky I was to capture such an unforgettable scene on my very first excursion!

This moving experience led me to search out every place from which I could view the peak. Knowing nothing of mountain climbing, I now began collecting mountaineering equipment. I commenced my climbing career with the three mountains of Shirane in Japan's Southern Alps. That night my tent was swept away in the tempestuous winds, and I was fortunate to live through the night by digging a snow shelter. How beautiful was the dawn of that frigid morning!

In this manner I have been losing myself for the past eight years. Each evening I left my Yokohama home and kept pressing the shutter throughout the night and morning, not returning home until past noon. After that I did my daily work. I continued this routine summer and winter all year round, having no other worldly cares.

During the last few years, however, I have become increasingly attracted to climbing Mt. Fuji herself, rather than merely seeking vantage points from which to view the mountain. In my climbs I have seen Mt. Fuji's volcanic rocks burnished red, volcanic ashes, masses of vegetation crawling over the ground, fields of wildflowers, seas of trees, mounds, wind holes, swamps, and the yawning crater. Each of these features, and a host of minute fragments, combine to create Mt. Fuji and to sustain her beauty. The contemplation of these many parts has profoundly altered my perception of the mountain.

There is, of course, no way to foresee how Mt. Fuji may change her appearance for me in the future. I can only hope to be able to continue to regard her face to face without being overwhelmed by her grandeur.

And finally, I should like to express my sincere gratitude to Mr. Makoto Ōoka, Mr. C. W. Nicol, and Dr. Hitoshi Takeuchi who have so kindly given of their valuable time to write for this, my first photographic collection. My thanks also to all the others who have been so helpful to me.

Autumn 1984